W9-BUE-104

THE ORPHAN BOY

B-1210
FT-010

A Maasai Story by

Tololwa M. Mollel

Illustrated by

Paul Morin

Clarion Books · New York

To my son, Lese.
– T.M.M.

To my parents, for first opening my eyes to Africa.
And to the Maasai of Masai Mara.
– P.M.

As he had done every night of his life, the old man gazed deep into the heavens. He had spent so much time scanning the night sky that he knew every star it held. He loved the stars as if they were his children. He always felt less lonely when the sky was clear and the stars formed a glowing canopy over the plains.

Tonight, he noticed, one of the stars was missing.

Like a worried father, the old man searched the darkness for his missing star. Just then he heard the sound of footsteps.

Startled, the old man looked down, and there before him stood a boy. "Who are you?" he asked.

"My name is Kileken," replied the boy. "I am an orphan and I've travelled countless miles in search of a home."

The man's eyes shone with excitement. "I am childless and live alone. I would be most happy to have you as a companion. You are welcome to live here as long as you want."

And, forgetting all about the missing star, the old man set to making a bed next to his own for the boy to sleep on.

When he woke up the next morning, many surprises greeted the old man. Waiting for him in his favourite bowl was steaming hot tea, made with lots of milk, just the way he liked it. The cows had been milked. The compound and the cattle pen had been swept clean. But Kileken was nowhere in sight. He had taken the cattle out to pasture.

In the evening when Kileken returned, the old man was waiting. "It takes me forever to do all the morning chores," he said. "How did you do everything in time to take the cattle to pasture by sunrise?"

The boy smiled a mysterious smile. "The day begins at dawn," he replied. "I get my energy from the first light of day." He chuckled. "Besides, I'm much younger than you are!"

The old man was still puzzled, but he decided not to ask any more questions. After all, Kileken had been a great help, and he was good company too. They spent the rest of the evening sitting quietly together out under the stars.

Just before going to bed the boy said, "We're almost out of water. I'll take the donkeys to the spring in the morning."

"Good," the old man replied. "While you do that, I'll look after the cattle."

The boy shook his head. "No, no. I'll fetch the water and take the cattle to pasture. As long as I'm here, I'll do all the work for you."

It was the old man's turn to chuckle. "Look, it takes two whole days to go to the spring and back. And it takes another day just to load the donkeys with water. That's a big job for a boy your size. You can't possibly care for the cattle if you're going to the spring."

Again, Kileken looked mysterious. "If you trust me, I can do it," he said.

By sunrise the next morning, the boy not only had fetched the water, but had done the morning chores as well. The cattle were out grazing by the time the old man woke up.

When Kileken returned in the evening, the old man stared at him in silent wonder. His mind burned with curiosity, but something about the boy stopped him from asking questions.

By and by, the rains fell and the land turned a glistening green.
The old man's heart was full of joy. His face became brighter and
his step more youthful.

Kileken continued to amaze the old man with his strange deeds. But though he was curious, he asked no questions. In time he regarded Kileken as the son he'd never had.

The rains were followed by drought. The sun hooked its claws into the soil and a flaming sky burned up the grass and dried up the spring. Buzzards darkened the sky, waiting for cattle to die of thirst.

The old man shuddered. He watched the circling birds and murmured, "If it doesn't rain soon, we will be dead."

"No, we won't die," the boy said, with a faraway look in his eyes.

The next evening, when Kileken came home from the pasture, the old man had the greatest shock of his life. His cattle were fatter and rounder than he had ever seen them.

The old man couldn't contain his curiosity any longer. "Kileken!" he burst out. "The drought has burned up the last blade of grass and the last drop of water. By the stars above, how do you bring the cattle home with their bellies bursting from good grazing?"

A little sparkle lit the boy's eyes. "It's something I learned from my father. He had a hidden power over the drought and he passed that power on to me. But it will work only as long as it remains my secret and mine alone. He told me never to reveal it."

Suddenly an urge to understand everything came over the old man. "Please, tell me," he pleaded. "You can trust me. I won't breathe a word of your secret to a soul!"

Kileken shook his head. "A secret known to two is no secret," he said. "I must not tell you and you must never seek to know. For the day you discover my secret will be the end of your good fortune."

The drought worsened. The plains echoed with the groans of dying beasts. But under the boy's care the old man prospered. More calves were born than ever before and there was more milk than even a growing boy could drink.

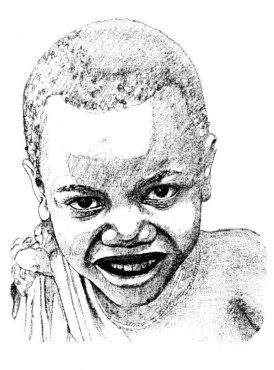

But as the old man's fortune grew, so did his curiosity. Each day his longing to know the boy's secret sharpened until he thought of nothing else. His face became clouded with worry and he seemed to age more than ever.

Unable to sleep one night, the old man sat by the fire. His shadow glared down at him from the wall of the hut. He watched as Kileken slept peacefully, and for the umpteenth time murmured to himself, "I wish he would tell me. I would give anything to know his secret."

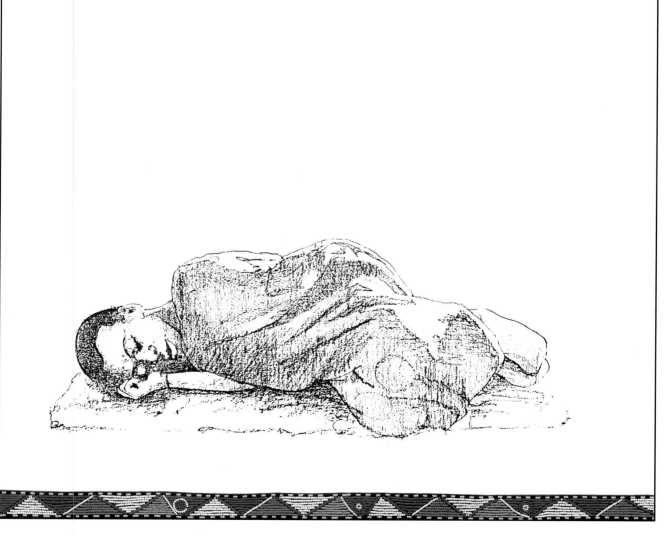

Suddenly a gruff whisper came from the wall. "Why don't you find out?" The old man was speechless as his shadow continued. "You could have found out long ago if only you had used your brains."

Excited, the old man whispered back, "What a fool I've been! Now, why didn't I think of that?" Then his face fell. "But I mustn't know. The boy . . ."

"Forget the boy!" snapped the shadow. "How long will you suffer

because of a silly little secret that a silly little child wants to hide from you? Besides, he doesn't need to know. You only have to be careful.''

For the rest of the night the old man plotted and planned. He would find out how Kileken worked his wonders. He would. By this time tomorrow, the secret would be his too. The boy would never know. He would be as sly as a jackal!

When Kileken got up in the morning, the old man pretended to be asleep. He lay still on his bed and listened to the boy's movements as he did the morning chores. Then the hut became quiet as Kileken herded the cattle out. The old man crept from his bed and followed at a safe distance.

The boy walked quickly with the cattle moving well ahead of him. When he was a good distance from the compound, he stopped. The old man scrambled for cover just in time. Kileken turned to look in all directions.

Satisfied that no one was about, Kileken climbed a rock and raised his arms. Instantly, the sun dimmed as a powerful glow spread down the boy's arms and through his body.

But from his hiding place the old man watched, and what he saw next took his breath away.

Suddenly, he was in the midst of magnificent waist-high grass, beautiful green woods and cool gushing springs. His cattle were drinking blissfully, their udders loaded with milk. A cry of wonder escaped his lips before the old man could stop it.

Kileken turned and saw him.

For an instant the boy looked into the old man's eyes. Gone was the trust they had shared. In its place was only sorrow.

The old man threw himself to the ground with a cry of despair and covered his face as the boy exploded into a blinding star. As he rose quickly into the air, the sun gradually regained its sparkle and majesty.

The old man stood up. Gone was the waist-high grass. Gone were the green woods and gushing streams. Gone were the fattened cattle with loaded udders.

There was only scrub land now, barren and drought-stricken. Thin, scraggly cows wandered about the parched countryside waiting for the rain that should come soon.

Lonelier than he had ever been in his life, the old man plodded slowly home. Waiting for him there in his favourite bowl was steaming hot, milky tea just as Kileken had made it that very first morning. But the hut was empty.

That evening, a lone star shone down from the west. Unlike other stars, it neither flickered nor twinkled. At dawn, ringed by the first rain clouds, it looked down from the east. The old man watched it in sad recognition. It was the star that had disappeared from the sky so many nights ago.

The night that Kileken came.

The star is the planet Venus. At dawn it appears in the east as the morning star. At nightfall it is the evening star in the west. The Maasai call it Kileken, the orphan boy, who is up at dawn to herd out the cattle after morning chores, and who returns to the compound at nightfall for the evening milking.

Clarion Books
a Houghton Mifflin Company imprint
215 Park Avenue South, New York, NY 10003
Text copyright © 1990 by Tololwa M. Mollel
Illustrations copyright © 1990 by Paul Morin
All rights reserved.
First published by Oxford University Press, Ontario, Canada
For information about permission to reproduce
selections from this book, write to Permissions,
Houghton Mifflin Company,
215 Park Avenue South, New York, NY 10003.
Printed in Hong Kong

ISBN 0-89919-985-3   PA ISBN 0-395-72079-6

10 9 8 7 6 5 4

Library of Congress Cataloging-in-Publication Data

Mollel, Tololwa M. (Tololwa Marti)
The orphan boy/by Tololwa M. Mollel: illustrated by Paul Morin.
p. cm.
Summary: Though delighted that an orphan boy has come into his
life, an old man becomes insatiably curious about the boy's
mysterious powers.
ISBN 0-89919-985-2
[1. Masai (African people)—Folklore.   2. Folklore—Africa.]
I. Morin, Paul. 1959–   ill. II. Title
PZ8.1.M730r   1990
398.21'089965—dc20
[E]
90–2358
CIP
AC